The MERMAID

JAN BRETT

G. P. Putnam's Sons

For my great-niece,
Ana Merrill

Thank you to Steven Bailey
at the New England Aquarium
and Sy, their Pacific octopus.

G. P. PUTNAM'S SONS
an imprint of Penguin Random House LLC
375 Hudson Street
New York, NY 10014

Library of Congress Cataloging-in-Publication Data
Names: Brett, Jan, 1949– author, illustrator.
Title: The mermaid / Jan Brett.
Other titles: Goldilocks and the three bears.
Description: New York, NY : G. P. Putnam's Sons, [2017].
Summary: "Set in the ocean off Japan, this retelling of Goldilocks and the Three Bears stars Kiniro, a mermaid,
who finds a baby octopus's breakfast, chair, and bed just right"—Provided by publisher.
Identifiers: LCCN 2016030386 | ISBN 9780399170720 (hardback)
Subjects: | CYAC: Mermaids—Fiction. | Octopuses—Fiction. | BISAC: JUVENILE FICTION / Fairy Tales & Folklore / Adaptations. |
JUVENILE FICTION / Animals / Marine Life. Classification: LCC PZ7.B7559 Mer 2017 | DDC [E]—dc23
LC record available at https://lccn.loc.gov/2016030386

Manufactured in China by RR Donnelley Asia Printing Solutions Ltd.
ISBN 9780399170720
1 3 5 7 9 10 8 6 4 2

Design by Marikka Tamura.
Text set in Winchester New ITC Std. The art for this book was done in watercolors and gouache.
Airbrush backgrounds by Joseph Hearne.

Under the sea, an octopus family got ready for a swim before breakfast.
"Time to put on your new hat, Baby," said Okāsan.

Baby did not like the floppy new hat.
The hat was not happy either.

As the octopus family set off behind their house, a little mermaid spotted their front door.

Kiniro had been drifting in a warm current with her puffer fish friend.

"Take care," Puffy warned. "You never know who may live there."

"But I'm so curious!" she said. Kiniro sashayed toward the seashell house.

Inside, breakfast had been set out. There was a great big shell,
a middle-sized shell, and a little shell.

Kiniro took a bite from the great big shell. "Too crunchy," she said.

The little mermaid tried the tender bites in
the middle-sized shell. "Too slimy," she said.

Puffy could guess what was coming next.

Kiniro sidled up to the little shell. In a minute the tempting tidbit had disappeared.

"Just right!" she said.

"All gone," said Puffy as he wondered whose breakfast it really was.

Kiniro floated around the seashell house and saw three chairs.
There was a big chair, a middle-sized chair, and a little chair.

She sat down on the large coral chair.
"Too many bumps," she said as she smoothed her scales.

Kiniro wriggled into the middle-sized chair. Down she went.
"This chair is too slippery," she gasped.

The little chair was the prettiest of all, and Kiniro sat on it.
"Just right," she said, and she gave her fins a flipperty flip.

All that wiggling broke the chair to bits.

Kiniro was sorry about the pretty chair, but not for long, because in the next room she spotted three beds. She and Puffy had been swimming for hours and were ready for a nap. She swam over and settled in.

"What sweet dreams we'll have!" she told her friend.
But someone had been eating in that bed, and there were
smashed shells and crab claws all around.
"This bed is too messy," she sighed.

She flopped down on the middle-sized bed. "This bed
is too squishy," she complained.
As Kiniro patted her tiara, she spied the last small bed.

It rocked like a cradle in the tide. She set her head down
on a pillow star and fell sound asleep.

Soon, the octopus family returned over the sandy shoals.
Right away, Otōsan saw his breakfast shell overturned. "Someone
has been crunching on my crustaceans," he said, turning pink.

Okāsan huffed, "My breakfast has been splashed!" She turned pinkish too. Baby looked around for her breakfast, but all she saw was the upside-down shell. "Someone has been eating my breakfast, and there is nothing left for me!" she cried.

Otōsan saw that his coral chair looked different. "Someone has been sitting on my chair!" he announced, now even redder.

Okāsan went from pink to red when she saw her chair. "Who has been squashing my chair and scattering my teacups?" she asked.

Baby saw her beautiful chair all in pieces. The hermit crabs
were taking it. "My chair is going, going, gone!" she cried.

Sensing something else was amiss, Otōsan squeezed into the bedroom.
"Someone has been sleeping in my bed!" He blasted ocean water and
kicked up the star-shaped sand.

Puffy felt the ripples as Okāsan jetted toward her bed.
The soft seaweed she liked to drowse in was tangled and torn.
"Someone has been sleeping in my bed," she said.

Baby Octopus peeked inside her tiny bed.

A beautiful mermaid was sleeping there.

"Someone has been sleeping in my bed, and here she is!"

The little mermaid opened her eyes and saw the adorable octopus. The baby's eyes were soft and sweet. Her skin was shell pink. Her graceful arms danced. But she was wearing the oddest hat the little mermaid had ever seen.

Kiniro, who didn't like to see anyone unhappy, gasped. "That will not do!" She thought about her tiara.

Just then, all three octopuses reached for Kiniro with their twenty-four arms.
Puffy was ready. He puffed with all his might.

Puffa-puffa, pokety-poke, stickety-stick! His sharp prickles did not let
the octopuses near the little mermaid.

Kiniro, Puffy, and their new friend, Ray, floated away in the warm current.
They couldn't stop smiling about the baby octopus.

She looked radiant in her beautiful new tiara.